Published by The Future Ancients.

lukalesson.com | thefutureancients.com

"I myself praise Eros and practice Erotics above all things
and I urge others to do likewise"

- Socrates, *The Symposium*

"Justice is what love looks like in public"

- Dr Cornel West

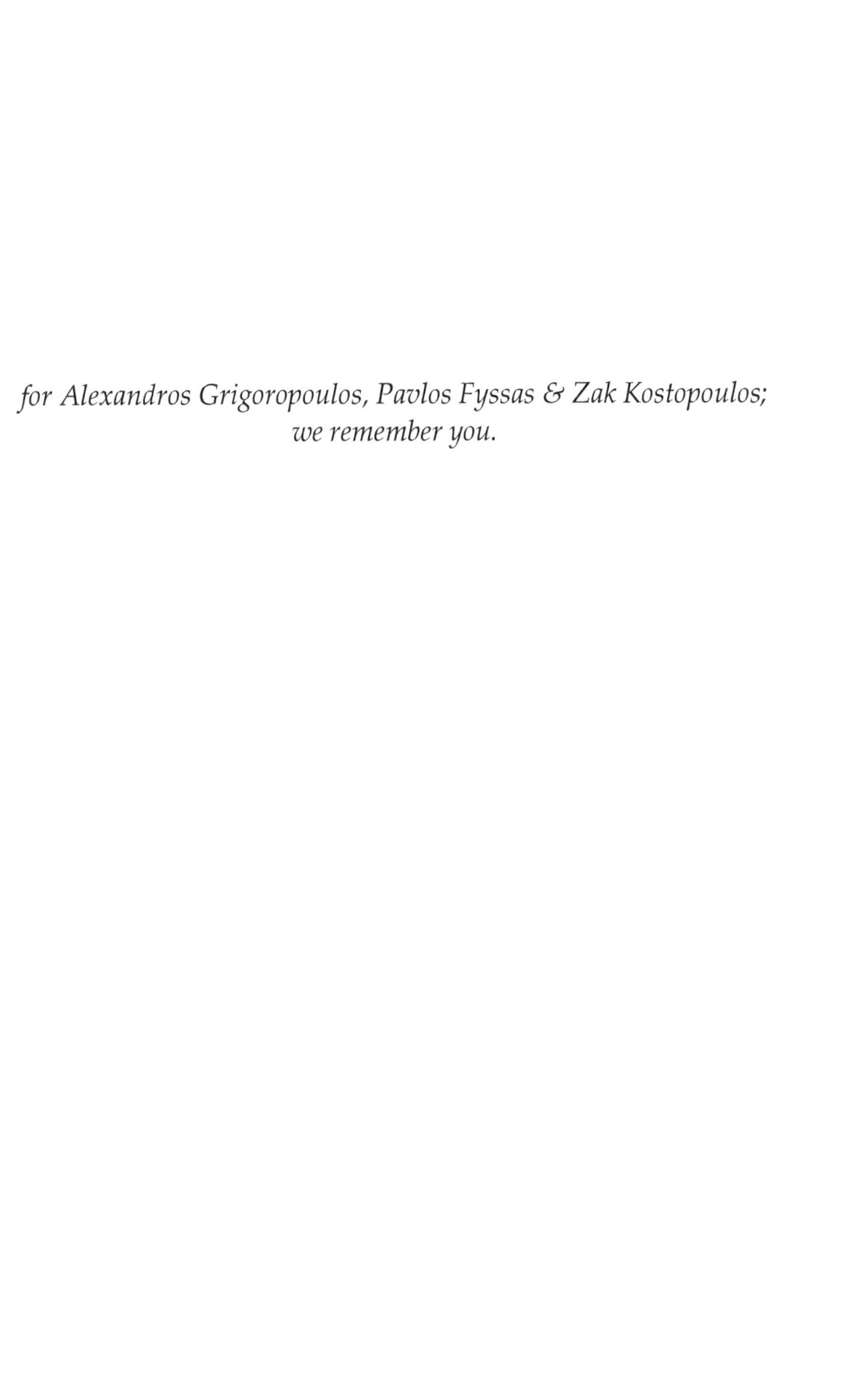

for Alexandros Grigoropoulos, Pavlos Fyssas & Zak Kostopoulos;
we remember you.

AGAPI

& OTHER KINDS OF LOVE

Introduction

This book has defied bushfire, a viral pandemic, two cancelled premiere seasons, two floods and a broken Arts sector in order to arrive into your hands. The seven different types of love this book deals with, all acted as guides as I maneuvered my way through the most intense years of my creative life – words like 'pivot', 'adjust', 'redefine' and 'reinvent' became ubiquitous around me, but somehow I was able to protect the pages of this book from being overtaken by them.

While I was told I should throw all my energy at becoming a tiktok star, I returned to the basics. I worked to remind myself of how I am nourished by this meticulous pen-to-paper process. At times, the distance between my pad and pen and your reading eyes could not have felt greater. Sometimes it felt like this manuscript was buried in a cave on an unscalable cliff in the northern reaches of the motherland or soaking in spew in a post-party gutter of Athens. Zeus knows, there were moments when this body of work was literally lying in the trash.

Agapi & Other Kinds of Love started as the title of a solo theatre show, co-commissioned by LaBoite Theatre in Brisbane and Bleach Festival on the Gold Coast. The first bits and pieces of writing and researching for the original co-commissioned show were undertaken in my wife's homeland of Chile. The depth of Chilean history providing me with a prism through which I could see reflections of so much of my homeland of Greece – the political landscape, the warmth of the culture, the anarchist streets of

Valparaiso reminding me of the back alleys of Exarcheia in Athens, and the poetic history howling with the rebellious hearts of peasants and protestors calling to love and be loved in return. The call of the downtrodden to be loved equally, just for one moment, by the state.

I thought of the case of Pavlos Fyssas aka *Killer P*, the Greek rapper who was killed by Neo-Nazi Golden Dawn supporters in cold blood one night on the outskirts of Athens. I was reminded of how the Low Bap music community in Greece responded – how they mourned him with music and concerts and strengthening the movement against fascist ideals even when they were crying for their brother.

I was reminded of the fact that, at the time, over 50% of all police officers in Greece were members of Golden Dawn; an openly fascist political party that had landed fair and square in the Greek parliament on an anti-immigration nationalist message. I thought of the time I spent with the founder of the music genre, Low Bap, a kind of hip-hop that leans on dark, lo-fi beats, focused on the storytelling and the bringing together of the political and the poetic. I thought about the police officers in their uniforms, and the anti-fascist Low Bap fans always wearing only black to concerts. I thought about how those concerts felt as much like political rallies or football hooligan gatherings as they did music gigs.

This then reminded me of a conversation I once had with the great African American thinker Dr Cornel West. We were backstage at his show in Sydney, which I was supporting at the time. We spent a little over 30 minutes unpacking his quote: "Justice is what love looks like in public" and how love is the way forward for justice movements. We talked about how love is a holy land of sorts. Love does not need to be soft, but we can fight vehemently for the things that we love, without dehumanizing the people we are fighting with. We also talked about the Greek music genre of *Rembetika* and how it is considered the 'Greek Blues'. In each sentence we spoke we found the commonalities between our people, and in doing so,

Dr West embodied his quote and showed me how it can be done, through conversation, through dialogue - one common thread at a time.

I chose the topic for this project because I wanted to learn more about the Ancient Greek types of love myself and the momentum was already upon me. By that time, I had read Plato's *Symposium* and had become obsessed with one particular gap left in the text. I became interested in a woman named: Diotima. In *The Symposium*, Socrates quotes her as being the one who taught him everything he knows about love. And yet, someone so important, someone who is said to have taught one of the greatest teachers and philosophers of all time, is mostly lost to us. We know very little else about this great woman, except for Socrates' mentioning of her. And that she is said to have held back the plague of Athens from hitting the city for ten whole years.

By this time, my wife and I decided to rent a house in my grandfather's village of Monolithos, Rhodes. Life on the island was spacious. Time moved slowly, we saw summer turn to winter, picked mushrooms in the forest behind the village and took them to the local Taverna – where the owner cooked them with pasta and chestnuts. We picked olives on my cousin's grove and spoke of heritage.

I started writing another book of poems there. For the first time in my life, I felt like I just couldn't be in that place and write of elsewhere. It wasn't fair. I felt like I'd be cheating on the village if I came to the people, sat with them, drank with them, passive-smoked with them, but went home to write of other people and other places. But I did start to see the loves around me more clearly.

I saw *Filoxenia*, in the way the locals had welcomed refugees into the village – given them jobs, places to hang, fair pay & and place to call home. I also saw how *Filoxenia* was lacking in some cases as well. Like on the nearby island of Symi, while the tourists buzzed around the port on a Disney-esque, motorised train, spewing a horrible version of Zorba the Greek into the air, a hundred refugees were hanging over the walls of the police station, living their lives in limbo, unable to settle there officially.

I saw *Pragma* in the village as well. Old couples looking almost like they were about to be cemented into place where they stand like marble statues. Some of them had been together more than 60 years, their thick hands cutting tomatoes with knives that have been sharpened so many times the blade is half the thickness of the handle. They know each other so well, they almost looked numbed to each other's presence – words not needing to be spoken, perfectly dancing around each other, just in super slow motion.

We spent New Year's Day, the coldest I'd ever seen the city, in Athens - I remembered how incredibly beautiful and how incredibly vicious Athens can be to those who live there. The city has bite. We spent time in Exarcheia, the suburb that features heavily in the book. We saw a cop car try to enter the streets of the suburb while a guy in all black hanging off the balcony of a known anarchist squat threw half a brick at them. It hit the car on the roof - he ran down the stairs to meet them head on as they sped off, the other half of the brick in hand, shouting obscenities, letting them know they are never welcome. Exarcheia is autonomous, it governs itself. Police still have a very hard time showing any authority there.

When we came back to Australia, bushfires had been through the country. Ashes lined the freeways; new shoots were starting to think about braving it, about poking their green heads out from the black crust. Again, I returned to *Agapi*. Getting ready to premiere the work at Melbourne Writers' Festival. It was February 2020.

You know the rest.

The following year we were booked to premiere at Brisbane Festival, this time with the addition of music composed by James Humberstone from the Sydney Conservatorium of Music, and two talented musicians accompanying the performance. James had come on board with a unified vision of a show that I believed could bring us closer together as a community, not split us further apart. He painstakingly researched Low Bap as a sub-genre of Hip-hop, as much as Ancient Greek instrumentation and the crazy marrying of these worlds through something more post-apocalyptic that I kept insisting on including.

Again though, the same story, that show was also cancelled.

In between these cancellations is where the show *Agapi & Other Kinds of Love,* really turned into this book you're reading. This book is not simply a copy of the script. It is a more expansive look at the world of Pavlos and Sophia, Socrates and Diotima and a deeper ode to the city of Athens; ancient and modern. Thanks to the very sharp eye of poet Omar Sakr, who looked through this text and provided edits and provocations, the script was able to be pushed further.

In the process of completing this book, my wife and I were blessed with the presence of our first child. Our son has brought with him so much to love. So much so that I don't think it would have been right for me to complete a body of work about love without first experiencing the love of a parent. Many of the months of writing of this book were paralleled by birthing classes, the post-partum bubble, sleepless nights, naps with a little prince lying on my chest, first teeth and tears and plenty of laughter. His presence and the presence of my wife as she transitioned into becoming a mother taught me so much about love. So much that I hope to find a way to name it in the future, but for now, it lives in between the lines of this book.

On a practical note, this book is meant to be read twice. Once completely ignoring the numbers linking you to the endnotes – as one flowing and enjoyable reading of the single narrative. And then once again, this time stopping to enjoy Chaos' Notes throughout to add another layer of depth.

A note for the passionate reader of history and Greek philosophy - I am not a historian; I am a poet. I've stolen the parts of history I find interesting or provocative and adapted them, extrapolated upon them, thrown them against the walls of the Parthenon, shaken the superfluous out of them and added my own style, aesthetic, ideas and politics and produced something not altogether new.

Με αγάπη

with love,

Luka 'Lesson' Haralampou

Appreciation

To my wife, Isa, I love you forever. To my son, Kyanos, the greatest of gifts – you mean the world to us.

Many heartfelt thanks to Omar Musa, David Stavanger, Petr Malapanis, Amir Paiss, Ally Michel, Konstantinos Kalymnios and Hanna May – for the conversations and time taken that contributed to completing this book.

A special shout out to Omar Sakr for his keen eye for detail, thank you for your time, brother. To Vyv Abla for believing in another one of my crazy ideas.

To my collaborators for this project at large: Sam Foster, James Humberstone, Greta Kelly, Ella Fence, Avishai Barnatan, Anita Kwong, Laura Jade and Jack Tierney – thank you for adding your time and energy to this body of work.

To my family and friends in the motherland; σας ευχαριστώ.

To the Molina-Bobba and Vagamundi families, we miss you and will be seeing you soon. To my Haralampou family; Mum, Dad and Eliah - thank you for all your support this year.

A special mention to the National Museum of Australia for hosting the premiere of *Agapi & Other Kinds of Love.* And to Bleach* Festival and LaBoite Theatre for originally believing in this work and co-commissioning the very first scribbles.

Chapter One
Χάος & Κόσμος | Chaos & Cosmos

In the beginning

    was not the word

before the word, there was a breath

        an open mouth

  from which Chaos[1]
    regurgitates:

      a snake

They spit a thick oil slick into the abyss

   a heaving mass
     of clay and blood

between the creases of their lips

  Chaos fabricates

the unworked dough of a universe

      poised

      on the edge

      of becoming

They hang in an empty void

    like a fat baby in the womb of history

  or the oily larva of a butterfly
          pinned in a black frame

as Cosmos[2]
  hovers beside them
  proud of their lover
  with a hand on their shoulder

from the thick mud of miracle

   they form cubes and spheres

  slowly
   the soft point of a pyramid
         rises under the heaviness

     the blunt peak of progress
        is birthed through a seething mass

Stalactites of basalt and silica
     harden
      and break
  from the serpentine river

As ουρανός[3]: the sky
  is thrown from the hands of Cosmos into the ether

shards of light
        are captured

    and wrapped

into tight pockets of combustion

                        and pitched

                                high into the dark

The earth is flicked like a marble

        into
                our
                        galaxy

And like the debris of a hurricane
                        flowing down a bursting river

all the great wonders of the world appear:

 the Twelve Apostles
        fall out like teeth from the jaw of the Grand Canyon

the Himalayas rise from the sludge
                        like the spine of a great whale

Reptiles and fish with their shimmering scales
                separate from mineral seams

        the muscle heavy tunas

                        pulled from pure silver

        the soft bellied river salmon

                        swim   from   rose   gold

Whole species explode

                into constellations of genomes and genealogy

As Chaos and Cosmos

with the strength

of their love

keep creating:

Fireflies that glimmer
     fire
     timber
     opposable thumbs and fingers
     as many summers as winters

Cats, Bengal tigers
     rhinos and elephants fighting
     the bite of a venomous spider
     scorpions, diamond pythons

Monkeys with their balance
     zebras and their patterns
     eagles and their talons
     flowing manes on wild stallions

Beetles and insects
     ants in their deep nests
     locusts that infest
     the first woman
     turns cow dung into incense[4]

Coal turns into diamonds
     bones become reminders

memories and inscriptions
Egyptians and Mayans

Calendars and astronomy
scavengers learn geometry
start pushing the parameters
of the patterns in ecology

Arrows and spears
turn to gallows and sneers
murders in the shadows
as open battles appear

Tribes rise and fall
allies fight the storms
divide and conquer
or devise and crawl

Pages and pens
make sages and trends
war is waged by invasion
through the ages and then...

Athenians start building columns
dragging marble from the bottom
to the top of the Acropolis
to honour their forgotten

Gold plated virgin
statuettes placed in their perches
eternal fires burning
buying spices from merchants[5]

Cutting pine to make altars
the meat seasoned and salted
they use mortar and pestles
to heal wounds with a poultice

They write on papyrus
    architects and designers
    measure the height of their marbles
    with the light of horizons

And so a city is built
    upon obsidian silt
    in the mouth of a volcano[6]
    that won't erupt for a million tilts

A table is built
    six chairs and their legs
    the timber turned and adjusted
    with dovetails and pegs

The food is prepared
    the wine is poured
    into terra-cotta vessels
    the divine is called

Six philosophers unite
    raising glasses to Dionysus[7]
    the meat cooked in honey[8]
    they sprinkle the final spices

Tonight[9], they'll talk honestly
    on philosophy and prophecies
    among them:
    Plato
    Socrates
    the playwright Aristophanes

They pause for a moment
    before Socrates speaks
    ready to bear witness
    to what the old sage thinks

His mouth opens
          with a breath
          along his tongue

          as he offers his thoughts on
                    how the universe was born from

                              Agapi
                                        and other kinds
                              of love[10]

Chapter Two
Εξάρχεια | Exarcheia

Socrates says:

"A woman: Diotima
   taught me I was enough
   taught me all about
   the ladder of love

First step
   Eros[11]
   then
   Storgi[12]
   and
   Filoxenia[13]

Fourth step
   Philautia[14]
   then comes
   Filia[15]

Sixth step
   Pragma[16]
   - a longer lasting love

Seventh step
   Agapi[17]:
   shine brighter than the sun[18]"

Although he wasn't reading from pages
    everything was perfectly stated

as he said:

"Throughout the ages
    people will sit at these tables
    and speak of love
    for all the moon's phases

While Athens will have fallen
    and risen[19]
    people will still sit and talk business
    argue over politics
    and their reasons for living…"

Chaos and Cosmos
reclining on their astronomical mattress
in a bedframe of constellations
switch from The Symposium

happening in the house of Agathon
        the poet
            Athens, 416BC

                to the same place
                    but in a different time…

            The city of Athens, 2022AD

And so it is that today
six citizens sit on milk crates
smoke cigarettes
   and discuss ways to escape

Athens is now melancholic
   crestfallen and chaotic
   full of lost souls
   alcoholics
   the painfully patriotic

They speak some philosophy
   but they're mostly gossiping
   five friends and that one cousin
   looking like he's lost again

Their names are
   Eleni
   Olympia
   their housemate
         Sophia

Stavros
   Giorgos
and his Greek-Australian cousin:

      Pavlos

They sit outside under a black and red star
   another Agathon[20] pouring Johnny Black at the bar
   the walls covered in tags and anarchist art
   in the cafe across the square[21] from the park

In the centre of Exarcheia[22]
   the heart of the protest movement

a block from the free clinic
    run by volunteer doctors and students

On the same stones Socrates walked
    back in the day
    some streets look the same
    but most buildings
                have decayed

They're surrounded by squats
    full of Antifa fighters
    a safe space for refugees
    the homeless
    and migrants

While neo-Nazis still have the nation divided[23]
    these citizens order cheap wine
                and reach for their lighters

Pavlos kisses Sophia
    on her cheek
    though he lowers his eyes
        when she speaks

            "Χάρηκα"
she says:

            "χάρηκα πολύ"

        Good to meet

He just stares at the street
    smiling through his teeth

It is December 6, 2022
    the anniversary of the night
      police opened fire
      killing a young boy[24]
      where he stood

The time hate
    did a drive-by
    on the neighbourhood

Every year on this date
    people gather
    in parks and on pavements

To protest the past
    state their truth to make sure
    their leaders don't become complacent

    they march and shout
      as we've always done through the ages

And as a crowd gathers in the square
    across the street
    Sophia learns why Pavlos
    hardly speaks

His cousin, Giorgos, tells her:

        "He isn't fluent in Greek
        he was born overseas
        a child of migrations
        and dreams"

So, Sophia switches to English

    catching him by surprise

She says:

> "Pavlos…
> I'm a pilgrim
>   a pilgrim…
>   on my own path
>   - What do you do?"

He says:

> "I'm a poet
>
> Sophia
>
> I guess I search for truth"

At that moment
    Socrates and Diotima fall in love again

Socrates and his teacher
            his lover
            his friend

Sophia and Pavlos:
            two reincarnations
            of the greatest
                    Ancient Greek lovers
                    that
                        ever met

Pavlos reaches out to touch her hand
    not knowing why
    just following his instincts

their invisible command

She sees it
    and knows what it is
            like she always did
her green eyes shining
    beneath her lashes and lids

At *that* moment
    the block fills with lines of police
    in their full riot gear
    arms locked in a V

As they fall in love
    and she strokes his arm at the crease
    the crowd rushes the cops
    like waves on a beach

And before they get caught in a flashback of past lives
            a local boy
    takes off his backpack
            ducks behind the front line

        pulls out two Molotov cocktails
                            and a light

        saying to himself:

    Fuck it
        it's my time to shine!

He flicks the flint and sets fire to the cloths

throws the bottles so high

that every clock in the city stops…

They land
and smash
right in front
of the cops
and it's *on*!!

Pavlos
shouts out at the top of his lungs:

ΤΡΕΞΕΤΕ!!

RUUUUUUUN!!

Chapter Three
Ἔρως | Eros

Chaos and Cosmos watch from above
   the riot
   that just kicked off in Exarcheia

Sophia takes Pavlos' hand
   and leads him through the backstreets
   into a stinking alleyway
   up some back stairs
   and inside her apartment

And for the first time
   in this lifetime
   the first kind of love—*Eros*
   takes hold…

Two palms grow hot like steel to a flint
   two hands touch
   sparks start to glint
   she opens the door
   and leads him in

      he closes his eyes, lets the dream begin

Outside the sirens
   call to the apartment
   screaming in the gutters
   winding in the darkness

An explosion hits three blocks away
   and it hums
      like a reverberating prayer

The city wakes up
   calls the fire brigades
   as Pavlos runs his hands through her hair

Their hearts start to burn
   as they turn in their feelings
   not thinking of the gas bottles
   in the bottom of the building

Or flames catching the foundations
   the water pipes growing hot
   her bedroom will be ablaze
   but for now

      their eyes are locked

        She's on top
      he's on top
     the top is lost[25]

She peels off the last layer
    double checks the door is locked

He holds her spine as she breathes him in
    admires her lines and the desires they sing

their souls start to crossover

        from the limits of their skins

Level 1 catches fire
    a window cracks
    ice melts off the roof
    dripping like wax

They didn't notice
    when the floorboards shook
    the first wave of smoke
    or the trembling books

Or the fire that flickered
    because their eyes did the same
    he spoke her name like a mantra
    on his tongue was a flame

He opened up
    forgot where he was
    she closed her eyes
    got lost with the gods[26]

Outside, another Molotov hits the pavement
    a cop car tries to get through the mazes
    a kid in a tracksuit and full balaclava

holds his crotch to the police in their full riot armour

Bottles fly as she bites on his shoulder
    her hair stuck with sweat
    as his touch feels older
    and known
    like a wayward soldier
    returned home
    who knows how to hold her

She touches him
    better than he touches himself

Sex becomes their language
    unwritten
    but eternally felt

She grabs the nape of his neck
            their rhythm increases

    their one breath[27]
        collapsing the past…

How beautiful

to fall in love

as the world

    falls apart

Later,
   they stare out the window
         as the room fills with smoke

Though neither is suicidal
      or thinks it's a joke

they both thought of dying in that moment

       - what a fucking great time to go[28]

He says:

   "I guess it's time to go"

They put on their clothes
    break out the window
    climb down the fire escape
    to the old road

The steel balustrade is hot
    but they hardly notice
    the tear gas already
    makes it hard to focus

A petrol-bomb bangs
against a bus on the block

     it burns
       like the sun

     right in front

       of the cops

Chaos and Cosmos
    switch back to watching Socrates
      with his thick beard
       and linen drapery

Telling the Symposium of 416BC
    how he met Diotima[29]
     on that silvery day
       in the Peloponnesian town of Mantinea:

"I saw her on a wooden bridge
        hung between two cliffs
        she stared right through my bones
        stole the pulse from my wrist

Eyes like full moons
        legs like the masts of ships
        we stood above the mouth of a river
        tongued by the ocean's rips

Crashing waves on the beach
        Poseidon's tides and reefs
        she spoke in gold leaf
        smiled with ivory teeth

I'd crawled those ragged shores
        leather sandals, tattered shawl
        she appeared in a cloud of light
        surrounding her flashing form

She walked like Hera danced
        when touched by Zeus'[30] hands
        fingers encrusted in stones
        smoked quartz and brazen hair

She was my welcome rest
        from the viciousness of men

an apparition set against
Athena's machines of death

She took me to her cave
    fires burning, candles, sage
    I kissed her temple's nave
    we touched with the lust of flames

I licked her spinal arc
    we danced in the lucid dark
    she kissed the whites of my eyes
    sucked the poison from my past

I sipped wine from her heart
    got drunk off the open cask
    high on her sacred sweat:

      - the nectar of the gods!"

And the men at the banquet
    swing their cups in the air
      singing:

      "Diotima
      the philosopher's[31] *priestess*
    Peloponnesian chieftess
      Gods wept when their lips met"[32]

Chapter Four
Η Ταραχή | The Riot

Back in Exarcheia, Athens, 2022AD

A wall of protestors

link arms

march

and scream:

"ΜΠΑΤΣΟΙ,
  TV,
  ΝΕΟΝΑΖΙ,
  ΌΛΑ ΤΑ ΚΑΘΑΡΜΑΤΑ
  ΔΟΥΛΕΥΟΥΝΕ ΜΑΖΙ![33]

THE COPS!
  THE TV!
  THE NEO NAZIS
  ALL THESE PRICKS
  HAVE THE SAME WET DREAMS!!"

Shit got heavy
  the students: angry and ready
  they rain rocks on the cops
  calling that shit *confetti*[34]

"WE'VE GOT A WAR
    FOR YOU MUTHAF*&#S
    WE'VE GOT A WAR!"[35]

Firebombs fall
    the tears of the poor

Sophia and Pavlos
    snap out of their dream
    duck for cover for a second
    before pushing through the streets

Exarcheia is on fire
    they cut through the cemetery
    past Kotzia Square
    and the statue of Pericles[36]

On every second corner
    there's a student on his knees:

"COPS BLOCK THE STREETS
        LIKE FREEDOM OF SPEECH!

            COPS BLOCK THE STREETS
                LIKE FREEDOM OF SPEECH!"

Past Syntagma Square
    heading for the old Mosque[37]
    past the ancient clock[38]
    and the boarded-up shops

They push forward
        running to the back
            of the Acropolis

                men run past wearing the masks
                    of Anonymous

red flares reflect
off a looming obelisk

the city looks like the dawn of an apocalypse

Sophia takes Pavlos
over the rocks

where they stop

atop

the hill of the Areopagus

Pavlos catches his breath
and says:

"We have to go back and fight
for the rights of the poor
for us—for equality for all!"

Sophia replies:

"We have to fight

but with love

because a loveless revolution
makes a future
not worth fighting for"

Chapter Five
Άρειος Πάγος I | Areopagus I

The Areopagus
is a rocky outcrop of granite and graffiti
perched just below the Acropolis
that overlooks the city of Athens

It's the meeting place of the elder's council
where justice was decided
    in ancient times[39]

And where Άγιος Παύλος, Saint Paul
brought the word of Jesus
to the Hellenic World[40]

On those historic stones
    Sophia calms Pavlos down
        with a long

                slow

            kiss

There they sit
    legs folded over each other in the dirt

In the distance
    they can hear firebombs exploding

The gravel
    vibrates beneath them
    like the pulse of a dying city
or the rebirth
        of a democracy[41]

Pavlos thinks to himself:

> *Sophia is so fearless*
> *always deep*
> *and coherent*

He says:

> "You know Eros...
> is my favourite god..."

Sophia raises an eyebrow:

> "Right...except Eros is *not* a god
> but a spirit who lives
> between us humans
> and the gods of Mount Olympus
>
> Eros - the carrier of love
> is a bridge between heaven and earth
>
> That's why when we pray with love
> our message is heard
> and when we pray with hate
> our message dies in the dirt
> never to return"

Pavlos' mind is burning:

> "So, Eros is a messenger like Hermes
> forever leaving and returning?"

She replies:

> "It's more liiiike…
> Eros is the oil in the engine
> or the ink for the poet
>
> He's not some sexy god
> all golden skinned and heroic
>
> Eros was born from a one-night stand[42]
> between Poverty and Abundance[43]
>
> That's why being in love makes us feel rich
> even when we have nothing
>
> On the flip side, love
> always wants to love *more*
>
> That's why we can have so much love
> but still feel
>
> love
>
> poor[44]
>
> Eros is the bridge between it all."

Pavlos stays silent
   as Sophia continues:

> "There are seven ways to know Eros
>   under the sun
>   something the ancients called:
>
> *The Ladder of Love.*"

Pavlos says:

"I've never known what love truly is
let alone these different types."

Sophia sighs:

"Well, the first love, *eros*,
is something you've already felt with me tonight...

but Pavlos –would you believe me if I told you
that I once met Aphrodite?"

Pavlos
looks her straight in her eyes
and says:

"I'm sure you have, Sophia
I'm sure you have"

Beneath the full moon that December

Sophia stands up

kicks off her shoes

pulls off her leather jacket

raises her hands to the wind

and starts to sing

Chapter Six
Στοργή | Storgi

"Τα ματόκλαδα σου λάμπουν βρέ

σαν τα λουλούδια του κάμπου

σαν τα λουλούδια του κάμπου βρέ

τα ματόκλαδα σου λάμπουν"[45]

I met Aphrodite!
   I did!

   But she wasn't the long
   flowing hair
   voluptuous
   curvaceous
   caramel-skinned type goddess[46]
   people think she is

But αχ Αμαν![47]
   - she is a god

See my Aphrodite
   was married to a strong man
   who worked the railroads

carving out rock from the mountain behind the village[48]
 laying tracks
 one steel peg
 one smack at a time

That was before the accident
            before WWII became a prequel
            before they started sending their donations
            before 'beware of falling rocks'
            became the family name
            before '10cm to the left and he'd have been okay'

Before my Aphrodite[49] came home
            to three young children and half a husband

Having one side of your body paralysed
   was one side too many for a mountain
   of a man like this

His children didn't take well to
half hugs
   half smiles
half murmured

                I love you's

But my Aphrodite did as true Aphrodites do
   year by year
   she fed him spoon by spoon

she showered and
   dressed him
   buttered his bread
   rolled his cigarettes

She brushed his teeth
   and hair

every morning
every night

and when they looked in the mirror…
she'd smile for both of them

                singing:

            Τα ματόκλαδα σου γέρνεις βρέ

                νου και λογισμό μου παίρνεις

                    νου και λογισμό μου παίρνεις βρέ

                τα ματόκλαδα σου γέρνεις

When their children left home
    Aphrodite still shuffled with him to church on Sundays
    where she'd sit him in the front row
    and he'd pray for a miracle[50]
    or at least ~~half~~ of one

She'd pray for time to go backwards
for stones
            to fall
                    upwards…

These days, us women pray
    in liposuction mantras
                to the cult of

    t h e   p l a s t i c   b o d y

honouring the toxicity of the male gaze

The goddess of love
   has been wrongly placed
      on the altar of impossible beauty

We have lost our knowledge
of the many kinds of love

Storgi[51] - this love
   only comes to us
     in times of great need

See this Aphrodite
   is my Grandmother, *Aphrodite*
   and her Hephaestus
   was my Grandfather, *Niko*

   and she looked after him all of his days until
   the good ~~half~~ of him
   finally
   p a s s e d   a w a y

So when you think of Aphrodite
   picture an 85-year-old widow
   who grew up a peasant
   and ended up a god[52]

Most of us
   wouldn't even know

~~the half~~

     of   it...

Chapter Seven
Διοτίμα στη Μαντινεία | Diotima in Mantinea

In 416BC, Diotima[53]
  at home[54]
    in the Peloponnesian town of
     Mantinea

kneels at an altar of Aphrodite Areia
        deep in prayer

She wraps herself in a linen shawl
dyed[55] by her own hands
lights the charcoal and the frankincense
    remembers the history of it all

She remembers a song
from years before
about a kind of love called

  Storgi

for the son[56] she once had[57],
    with the great philosopher

        Socrates

She picks up her Phorminx[58]
    settles on the floor
    and strums the first chords:

"My son,
    you're just the size of a sesame seed
    a grain of sand landed on your ancestors' beach
    but I want to take time out to teach you
    about a love called *Storgi*

See
    your family is from Athens' streets
    on Baba's side at least
    a place of philosophy and tragedy
    comedy and catastrophe
    and phoenixes rising from ashes

And gods and logic and passion
    laws and factions
    love and all its distractions
    and φιλότιμο[59]
    and many other things that I'll teach you in good time

And son
    though your life has hardly begun
    I wanted to teach you this old concept
    to help you through the contests of life…"

She sings the chorus:

"Storgi is a kind of love
        that will hold you and guide you, love

that will feed you and mind you, love
that will teach you to rise above..."

She strums into the second verse:

"Now you're just the size of a pomegranate seed
    hanging fruit on the family tree
    but I want to take time out to teach you
    because to teach you, is to remind me

This love
    will hold my hand as I hold your hand
    teach me how to teach you and
    stand beside me, as I give birth to you
    and you take your very first breath

The kind of love
    that'll make Mama
    wipe your mouth when you dribble
    make me want to frame your very first scribbles
    no matter how hard it gets
    I'll still want to hold you and kiss you

And forgive you your tantrums
    teach you your ethics
    and the temple's anthem:

        to love and be loved
        is to fall and be heard
        to heal and move forward
        with what you have learned

A kind of love
>   that gives shelter in the rain
>   lifts us out the puddles and the pain
>   a love that sustains

The love of the carers and servants
>   of being in service
>   to a much greater purpose."

She moans to an empty room:

"Στοργή is a kind of love
>   *that will hold you and guide you, love*
>   *that will feed you and mind you, love*
>   *that will teach you to rise above"*

She keeps strumming, gliding into the third:

"Now you're the size of a watermelon
>   shaded by the vine of the goddess and me
>   and I want to take time out to teach you
>   how love returns, eventually

See
>   when my time is done
>   and you're all grown up
>   and I'm old and grey
>   and my back is hunched

Remember this love…
>   *…remember this love*
>   *my son*

When you wipe my mouth as I dribble
    try to decipher my very last scribbles

Finish my sentence
    give me medicines
    take me on walks
    and forgive me my madness

This love
    will hold your hand
    as you hold *my* hand
    teach you how to teach *me* and
    stand beside you
    as you stand next to me

    and I take my

        last

            breath"

Diotima

    wipes tears from her face

        places her instrument back upon the altar

            and steps away from memory…

                She puts on her leather sandals

                    ready to walk on foot

towards

the illustrious city

of Athens

She hasn't seen Socrates for a long while now

but she's decided that it is time

to look him dead in the eyes

and see who she finds

Chapter Eight
Άρειος Πάγος II | Areopagus II

Pavlos leans against a giant stone of the Areopagus
    admiring Sophia's song
                    thinking to himself

> *There is nothing sexier*
>   *than a Greek woman*
>   *dancing a Zembekiko*[60]
>   *and singing*
>   *with her eyes closed*

By this time
    a crowd had gathered on the Areopagus

Students with bottles wrapped in paper bags
    a man and his street dog curled up on their stuffy blankets

Even some protestors
    tired from the night's fighting
    covered in tear gas
    and the milk
    they used to wash it off their faces

And the kid who threw the first Molotov cocktail
    he's there
        smoking a cigarette
        with his hoodie pulled up

lying on his back with his friends
    laughing
        at the moon

Aristocles[61]
    is a squat dweller
a Low-Bap[62] rap fan turned weed seller
  who volunteers
     at the local homeless shelter

His grandparents were advocates
   his parents were polytechnic student activists[63]
     so now he is an anarchist
       turned masked antagonist

Sophia says:

       "You know, Aristocles
       believes so deeply in *Filoxenia*
       that while most of his crew[64]
       are out drinking beers
       he's challenging the state
       making its hate disappear"

Pavlos responds:

       "*Filoxenia* - the love of the stranger"

Sophia replies

       "Κάτι ξέρεις, Παύλο μου
       Bravo! You do know something!

       Filoxenia - the love of the other
       of those most in danger"

Pavlos takes a deep breath
  and halfway through the exhale, says:

        "We're always so vexed
            with one-another
            even when we die
            they won't even bury us
            next
            to one another"

Pavlos breaks from Sophia's arms
    stands up and calls out to the people sitting on the Areopagus

  They all slowly
            start to pay attention
  lifting their heavy heads
      from their bottles and conversations

He asks each of them
    to hum a simple melody

walks around and shows them
    one by one:

            a-hum-hum-mmm
            a-hum-hum-mmm

Soon the night air is full of warm voices
    of this rag-tag bunch of loners and lunatics
    each with their own harmonies:

  a sound-bed of music fit for the Herodeon[65]

Pavlos calls over their humming and says:

        "Ok! Are you all ready!?"

(they nod their heads
        while trying not to lose concentration)

Pavlos
        rolls up his sleeves
                        takes a deep breath

        waits for a four-bar cycle to come back to the one

                        and speaks

        like a rap version of
                        Saint Paul

                - the apostle of hip-hop

                speaking the Good Word

                                to the pagans[66]

Chapter Nine
Φιλοξενία | Filoxenia

Pavlos raps:

"Bury me as a peasant
    no jewels
    no decadence
    don't mind if it's beneath the olive trees
    or the pediment

As long as hatred's irrelevant
    prejudice isn't prevalent
    we all look the same
    as skeletons in the sediment

White chipped bones
    high pitched moans
    maybe that'll mean the end of it

With our names set in stone
    they'll realise I meant it when I said:
    it's up to *us* to set the precedent

Red wine bullets
    pomegranate seeds
    sprinkled on my feet

Speak from the pulpit

in Arabic and Greek
bury us together with the same eulogy!

'Cause every cemetery

    has   a   separate   section

        for every sect

   They separate us in life

      They separate us in death!

Bury me next to the oppressed
   everyone our systems failed to protect
   when I take my last breath

   filoxenia!

Bury me at sea when the waves get rough
   watch me sink to the bottom with the storms[67] above

    and if they
   turn
     back
   the boats
     to lock 'em up

My ghost will scream:

  φιλοξενία!

'cause we are *them* and they are *us*

and we all look the same

when we turn to dust

that's love…

…*Φιλοξενία*""

The people on the Areopagus
inhabited by the spirits embedded in those sacred stones
spontaneously shout back to him:

"Oh Hades' caves!

ποιος θα αγαπάς - και ποιος θα μισείς;

πόσο μίσος μπορείς να κρατήσεις;

Who will you love and who will you hate?

How much of that hate will you take to your grave?[68]"

Chaos and Cosmos
resting their luminous forms
on a nebulous cloud of dust
switch channels
back to 416BC

Socrates has the guests at the Symposium
banging the same beat
with their feet
and fists
humming the same melody

a-hum-hum-mmm
a-hum-hum-mmm

Socrates opens

his mouth:

"The Spartans
they look just like us
they bleed and cry and die like us
they have wives and children and lives like us
and under their armour[69]
they just wanna survive like us

I don't believe that just because I am a proud Athenian
I should want to kill and take the fields[70] off the Elysians
joke about Kytherians
hate the Sirisians
overthrow the Rhodians
invade the Corinthians

I will not do the state's bidding for obedience
the reason is
we can do better than those previous:

Just because the Titans
       were overthrown by Olympians[71]
       doesn't mean we need to blindly follow
       violent precedent

I used to show the city my respect
       pray to Athena
       from the Parthenon steps

       sharpen my spear
       aim at their necks:
       all I got on return
       was a gut of regret

The state doesn't care about proof
       doesn't mind if the reason for war
       isn't true
       as long as it's a good enough excuse

       to take their fill
       to act with hate
       to rape and steal

But we must liberate and heal
       leave no stone unturned
       no dirt untilled

To play the long game
       until the proof distils
       to use our wills
       to unite and build
       until the truth's revealed

And hold no enemy
       no grudge against no man, no entity

I fight against signs of supremacy
        zealotry
        ignorance
        jealousy

        my word
        –my weaponry

That's my destiny:
        amplify empathy
        from Thebes to Thessaly
        I speak my elegies

Let our legacy

        be love:

because: we are *them* and they are *us*

    and we all look the same

        when we turn to dust"

Chapter Ten
Ἄρειος Πάγος III | Areopagus III

The full moon
  has a shimmering blue hue
    reflecting across its surface
something the ancients called: *Kyanos*[72]

  It hangs in the sky
    illuminating the Areopagus
    as the people give Pavlos

        a long
            slow
               clap

Half of them didn't understand a thing he rapped
               - just appreciated the vibe

They return to their conversations
  taking swings and puffs
  shuffling closer to each other
      as the night grows colder

Sophia kisses Pavlos on his neck[73]
  they stare into each other

      kiss
      and stare

and kiss again[74]

as only fresh lovers know how:

the world around them
          disappearing

Sophia says:

>   "Sweet Pavlos
>   all of that togetherness talk will make you a target
>   - you'll be stopped
>   before you even get started"

Pavlos replies:

>   "I know, but
>   I'd rather die for my art
>   than stay silent
>   and tell lies to my heart"

She says:

>   "I'm sure you would
>   but remember:
>
>   Self-love is a dying art
>   not
>   dying for your art"

>   That's the fourth step on the *ladder of love*:

>   *Philautia—*

>   Self-love"

Chapter Eleven
Φιλαυτία | Philautia

They look into each other's eyes
        from the silence Pavlos asks her:

                "Do you,
                Sophia

                Do you
                actually

                love

                yourself?"

Sophia smiles:

                "I know I love myself, Pavlos
                because I almost
                took my own life once

                but then…

                I didn't."

Pavlos holds her
        stares over her shoulder into an old olive tree
    bristling in the wind

the silver sides of its leaves
        flashing like a million tiny tongues

He says:

                "Me too!

                I mean…

                me either, Sophia

                I didn't kill myself
                        because I knew
                        to some friends
                        the end of me
                        would have meant
                        the end of them
                        too"

                "Well, sweet Πάυλο"

She says:

                "Sometimes our self-love
                saves the lives of others
                if we teach them how we love ourselves
                we can watch our self-love double

                that is the power of φιλαυτία…"

Pavlos

repeats the word to himself

as though it was a question:

"Philautia...?"

The word reverberates

through time and space

The dirt beneath them vibrates

as Chaos and Cosmos

dive deep into Pavlos' cerebral cortex[75]

to show him what that kind of love truly means

Pavlos sees

the Goddess Artemis
touching herself deep in the forest[76]
wearing nothing but a sheen of sweat
her eternal tan
and a thin rope with a shard of Amethyst
hanging between her breasts

A fawn
licks her toes as she comes

she moans: "φιλαυτία"

A boy, too young to be in the streets rioting
    just drew liquid pearls from his loins
        for the third time in an hour
while looking at photos of Freddie Mercury

His eyes rolling back in his head
        everything fading to white[77]:

        he whispers himself to sleep: "phiLAuTia..."[78]

The homeless man's dog, *Loukanikos*[79]
    who's been chewing on a bone under his blanket
        for two hours non-stop
      finally arrives at the sweet rotting marrow at the centre

    he growls: *"Phirruria"*

Aphrodite Areia
      the goddess of love, is thinking of her lover, the god of war

                  She ties up the leather straps of her bronze breastplate
places her festooned helmet onto her pretty head

      She has learned from him
                  that their love is worth protecting
                  that love cannot be made between two beings
                        in a house
                              under siege[80]

she flashes her teeth into the reflection of a polished shield

      Demanding:

                  "φιλαυτία"

Pavlos' Yiayia, back in Melbourne, is in her kitchen eating baklava-
filling by the spoonful

    while her family

  waits for her to bake a fresh tray

      She rests her hip against the kitchen bench
closes her eyes
  and takes in another mouthful

    she sings to herself while masticating[81]:

      "P h i l u ff t i ii a"

Pavlos' Pappou, in his favourite orange cardigan
is playing backgammon in front of a geriatric crowd
at the *Kafeneio*[82]

he slams his *Tuvli* piece on the board

He's been playing the whole game safe

and has finally taken the lead

over his long-time arch nemesis:

Kostas *the malaka*

he grunts to himself:

"Philautia *re gamoto*[83]"

Chapter Twelve
Διοτίμα στην Κόρινθο | Diotima in Corinth

Diotima
  on the long walk from Mantinea to Athens
     stops
    to pick a fig
      from its branch

  She pulls at the skin with her teeth

She remembers her old lover
  wonders if his hands have
    become calloused
      by battle
      or softened by prayer

she thinks:

    the philosopher's hands were always too soft[84]

She arrives at the city of Corinthos

    wanders past the leather maker's sandals
        hanging on a wooden frame

past the weaver's houses
    their looms hanging heavy with coloured thread

    Corinthos

      smells of a mix of rose water
          flowering geraniums
        and wild sage

      Chestnuts
      and quails
    roasting over open flames

    Diotima hears the shouts of drunken men
      playing κότταβος[85]
        behind a sandstone wall

She stops at the butcher's stall
       with its livers and ribs
     chicken feet and speckled eggs

  The butcher
    recognises her as a priestess of the temple[86]

    he asks her
   if she is available that evening

    for a fee

Diotima smiles
      looks the butcher in the eye
and points at the tongue of an Ox
        lying limp on the table

    he stays quiet

She pays without speaking

  carries the tongue like a baby in her arms

  up the hill, towards the temple on the Acropolis of Corinthos[87]

Diotima enters
		sees
			the statue of the goddess
	in her golden armour
				spear at the ready
	frozen—
	admiring her famous beauty
			in the reflection of her own shield

her eyebrows sharp

			teeth clean
				eyes
					solid stone

	She

				kneels on the cold floor

				and places the Ox's tongue

				at the foot of the goddess

On the Areopagaus

Pavlos is staring blankly into the darkness
           watching vignettes replay in his head

As all this *Philautia*-talk has reminded Sophia

        of a sweltering summer in high school

when her class visited the decaying skeleton of a temple

            perched on top of a hill

And the nerdy tour guide with a Greek flag on his hat

              told the group:

    "The Aphrodite worshipped here was

          Armed Aphrodite:

       The goddess of love, who was in love
          with Ares, the god of war

          Aphrodite Areia

     She was honoured by the Corinthians
         for teaching them
         that they were all worthy of protection
         and that
         Φιλαυτία, Self-love
         was the first line in their defences"

Sophia looked around at the rubble
    imagining the temple and its sanctuary

          "The temple housed a thousand worshippers"

He continued:
          "…followers of the goddess

disciples of the erotic arts

Their job was
to heal the wounded hearts

to
lick
the wounds
of Ancient Greece

It is because of these women
soldiers were healed
merchants returned year after year

And the city of Corinthos
was as rich as Athens

and they didn't

    have to wage a single war

to make their city prosper"

Chaos and Cosmos watch

Diotima lean against a column
    of the Temple of Aphrodite in 416BC

and Sophia
    against a stone at the Areopagus in 2022AD

Diotima looks up at the marble face of Aphrodite—

Sophia stares up at the moon—

they think to themselves:

I hope
Socrates
loves himself enough
to stand beside me as he is
not under me like a child
or over me like a pig

I hope he has learned

I hope
Pavlos
loves himself enough
to stand beside me as he is
not under me like a child
or over me like a pig

I hope he has learned

Φιλαυτία

so we can be bound together
by choice
not by control
or jealousy
or fear

so we can be bound together
by choice
not by control
or jealousy
or fear

Diotima closes her eyes

as the Ox's tongue

slow as a leech

finds its way to the ankle of Aphrodite

slides up her sculpted thigh

slurps the line of her marble spine

sucks around her cold neck

and rolls its way
into her open mouth

where it settles

hardens—

turns to gold

Chapter Thirteen
Πϱάγμα | Pragma

Chaos rests their intergalactic silhouette on the shoulders
    of the seven sisters
    they yawn
    and a galaxy disappears

As popcorn kernels the size of Saturn
    pop their thunderous explosions
    in a black hole besides them

Cosmos
    sick of all this sappiness, crunches on a planet
    and switches the channel
      back
        to the Symposium
          of 416BC

Socrates
    with his beard covered in breadcrumbs and olive oil
    is holding his terracotta *kylix* of wine in the air
        loudly lamenting
    a kind of love called *Pragma*:
      a long-lasting love, he never had:

"Our shadows danced on the cave wall
        a metaphor for our great fall
        silhouettes of our full selves:
        fate never called us to take form

I prayed to Themis
        surely our love could be made Law

I called out to Zeus
        he just wanted her as his escort

She said:
        'Socrates, love is a spark'

I said:
        'So, follow me into the dark'

She said:
        'No, no, love is a bridge'

I said:
        'then, Διοτίμα, lead us across this ditch'

    I prayed to Artemis
        surely she could hunt love down
        I was sure she could shoot silver arrows in the forest
        pin those lips to my open mouth

    We could have grown old together
        could have felt the unity of souls together
        could have felt our old bodies fall apart
        as our spirits only fused closer together

    We could have met the chambers
        of each other's old open hearts
        instead, we became strangers

I dance with a shadow of the past

We could have felt Πράγμα:
>   her presence - my only panorama
>   our connection only getting stronger
>   getting old
>   as a symbol of honour[88]

She said:
>   'Our future is dark'

I said:

>   'Only as dark as the shadows we cast'

>   I still sip wine from her heart
>   get drunk off her open cask

>   get high on her sacred sweat
>   I still get high off her sacred sweat

>   I still get high…"

Socrates is searching,
  looking into the sky for a sign

>   "I remember when

>   she was

>   *the nectar of the gods!"*

    The men at the table raise their voices:

"Diotima
the philosopher's priestess!
peloponnesian chieftess
Gods wept when their lips met!"

They Sing!

"Diotima
the philosopher's priestess!
peloponnesian chieftess
Gods wept when their lips met!"

They Sing!

"Diotima
the philosopher's priestess!
peloponnesian chieftess
Gods wept when their lips met!"

They Sing!

Socrates throws himself back into his chair
    nursing his heavy head

Alcibiades
    Socrates' once-young-student-turned-long-term-lover
    is jealous of his loud proclamations for this

Diotima

He holds Socrates' hand
    stroking his fingers:

    "It is over now, Socrates

    she left *you*, remember?"

Socrates looks at him
    with a guilty resentment

    "She never told you why

    and you never miss her when you're sober"

Chapter Fourteen
Ἄρειος Πάγος IV | Areopagus IV

Cosmos is watching a billionaire businessman
in his over-exaggerated phallic symbol of a rocket
           sail right past them

They pluck him from the air
     use the rocket to tickle Chaos for a minute
                 before
                    throwing it into the sun

Just as Sophia says:

          "Pragma – it's a love that's pragmatic
          it's all-the-more automatic
          it's an old couple
          that knows each other's bad habits"

Pavlos asks:

          "How do you know all of this stuff?"

Sophia says:

"From the Symposium on love
 of 416BC

Plato said it was the greatest meeting of minds
that he ever did see

But it was really just a group of men
eating like pigs
tickling each other's balls
getting drunk
and talking shit"

Pavlos laughs, pink as hell.

They hold each other

> look out across the city
>> with its flickering lights

> the dark hill of Lycabettus[89]
>> stares back at them
>>> with its heavy shoulders

The view of the Agora[90] below
>> is hindered by smoke
> billowing
from a flare
> lying on the train line

>> spilling its confession onto the tracks—

> *this place has been fought over before*

A dulled cacophony hangs in the air
>> of a fierce riot in the distance

> an explosion in Exarcheia

> a siren burns through Θησείο[91]

> and below them

>>> a muffled scream

Eventually Pavlos says:

"I wish we were still talking shit
with our friends
it's been a while since we got separated
and I haven't heard anything from them"

Sophia pauses
smiles
and says:

"Bravo Pavlos! *Filia*[92]
the kind of love that is endless
something called *friendship*

You can't survive this city without it

No doubt they're up to no good
but as long as they stick together
–they'll be ok"

Pavlos and Sophia stare into the distance

as the street dogs and wild wolves of Athens

start to howl

a haunting dirge

Near Syntagma Square
    Pavlos' cousin, Giorgos
    is helping his friend, Stavros
    across the street

       Stavros' skull has been hit by the baton of police

    his balaclava-clad head
    coated
      in thick ruby red

As the crowd
    of protestors and anarchists
    that have been fighting all night alongside them

         bang their sticks, baseball bats
           and shopping trolly bars

              on the road beneath them

    It is a beat

      that dents the bitumen

      that makes the people

        also turn their heads

          up to the moon

          and sing

Chapter Fifteen
Φιλία | Filia

"The city's on fire...

        the people in a rage

The city's on fire...

        there's no way to escape

You will not
        survive

    the flames

        without a friend on the way..."

Giorgos lays Stavros' heavy body down on the concrete

    rests his bloodied back against

        the tomb of the unknown soldier

  He holds
      Stavros' head in his hands
        and tells him:

"File[93] I'd die for you
    take a place in paradise for you
    as I take out a cigarette and light for you
    take one last puff of this life, would you

Remember when we used to
    drive up the top of *Lycabettus?*

    how the fuck we end up with nothing
    when we live in a city
    that used to have it all?

They called us
    the greatest of civilisations
    just another false 'civilised nation'

Where our civil rights became a living nightmare
    replaced by guards and barricades
    replaced by fascist serenades
    replaced by blood upon the pavement

But I'll never find a replacement
    for your friendship
    in these trenches

We used to smoke *nargile*[94]
    and place bets
    just before the crisis
    now I can't afford a pack of Marlboro Reds
    and every day is a roll of the dice

I knew we shoulda took off
    grabbed the cash you had hidden in the shoebox
    strapped the *mihanaki*[95] with the boombox
    and cruised towards our true north

Now the city's on fire
     pipe bombs and barbed wire
     pour the *petrelaio*[96]
     burn every liar
     spark up a flint
     light up them tires

The city's on fire
     we make the birds circle up higher
     make the dogs run from gun fire
     turn parliament to a funeral pyre!

Do you remember when
     we were just kids playing in the streets of Athens?
     everyday you'd try to steal my kicks
     rub my face in the fireplace ashes

Now we're side by side in the cauldrons
     fighting fire with fire in a war zone
     they don't know the coals that we've walked on
     to make sure our dreams aren't orphaned

This morning you woke up angry
     so you stole my old balaclava
     the one the cops know as my armor
     – the one that would make you a target

This morning you woke up living
     took my old balaclava
     who's gonna tell your mama
     I'm the one that should have been martyred?"[97]

The people
　　gather around the lost boys
　　　　holding their weapons in the air
　　　　　and sing:

"The city's on fire...

the people in a rage

The city's on fire...

there's no way to escape

You will not

survive

the flames..."

Stavros struggles to speak

     as Giorgos

  presses their foreheads together,

     smearing his friend's blood on his face

He knows you
     can't give
         mouth   to   mouth

    to democracy

    but still kisses Stavros

    on his swollen

      bloodied   lips

    through the hole of his own balaclava[98]

Along the edges
  of Syntagma square
  waves of anarchists
  join with the *bougatsa*-blubber stomachs
  of the taxi drivers' union

  in a face-off with the national guard

Two Pakistani youths
  Hasan and Adeel
   are standing on the corner
    next to their stolen shopping trolley
   turned shopfront

They aren't there to wage war, choose sides

  shout slogans

   or light fires

They're just there to sell

  a bottle of water

  a SIM card

  or a carton of milk

  to anyone

   who might want one

Chapter Sixteen
Διοτίμα στην Αθήνα | Diotima in Athens

In 416BC
	Diotima is taking careful steps
			as she approaches the Symposium
		happening in the house of Agathon, the poet

She takes a breath

	clicks her tongue against the roof of her mouth

	before she walks through the open door

past the sweating chefs

		labouring over a pot
			of steaming ducks

She hears his voice

		and follows it
		stepping over crushed flowers
			passing behind

	two half-naked men
				devouring each other
		in an empty corridor

she floats up the steps
         into a courtyard of columns
              and climbing roses

Outside
   she sways her way
         towards the head of the table

   where Socrates, mid-sentence, chokes on his words

         like they were chicken bones

   looks into his cup of wine for an answer—

              All the men fall silent.

the great philosopher

is

speechless

Diotima peels the cup away
          from his frozen hand

     She holds it high into the sky and says:

          "Love is a dream
          sweet Socrates:
          so, a toast to what we could have been!"

Diotima drinks
          and kisses Socrates on his stunned lips

As the drunken guests at the table
          throw their cups in the air and cheer:

          "Diotima
          the philosopher's priestess!
          Peloponnesian chieftess!
          Gods wept when their lips met!"

Plato kisses Aristophanes

     Eryximachus tongues Phaedrus

               Agathon pashes Pausanias

and Alcibiades

     just

     tongues the back of his hand

Diotima looks at Socrates,

    eyes full.

Half-drunk

    Socrates tries to sing their song

        through his wine-stained lips

      though his heart is an explosion

        his mouth: a fallen empire

    and his voice

      a beautiful rubble

                Like love
                    even when a song has been lost
            a fragmented melody still remains

Cosmos presses pause
    rolls over and touches Chaos in a way
      that creates a new solar system

Chaos smiles
    and a shower of asteroids fall over Venus

And that is why

      this is all we have left of the Song of Lovers[99]:

Socrates' verse:

"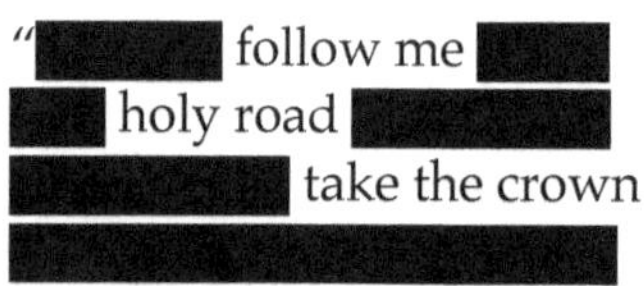 follow me
holy road
take the crown

Come, follow 
to nowhere
lay my head on
your chest"

      And Diotima's reply:

" carve out in stone

into my skin
"

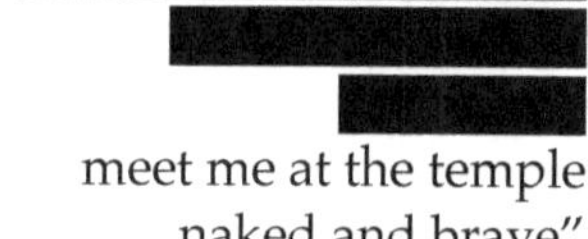

meet me at the temple
naked and brave"

A verse sung together:

> "Swim ▮ shore
> ▮ burn the bones ▮
> warm, warm ▮ soul
> ▮

> Run to the border
> ▮
> with you I'll go ▮
> ▮"

A final chorus:

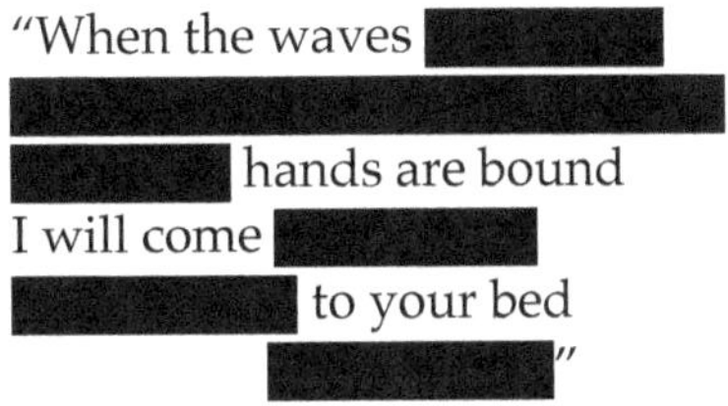

> "When the waves ▮
> ▮
> ▮ hands are bound
> I will come ▮
> ▮ to your bed
> ▮"

Chapter Seventeen
Ἄρειος Πάγος V | Areopagus V

Meanwhile, on the hill of the Areopagus

Pavlos, with his own cracked lips

plucks up the courage
to speak to Sophia
in his broken Greek

He asks her:

"*Sophia, dose mou ena filakì*"

But instead of saying *filàki*

he says: *filakì*

with the emphasis on the wrong syllable

(instead of asking for a

little kiss

he asks for a

little prison)

Sophia laughs
            walks off to sit with Aristocles, the Molotov cocktail kid

She swigs wine from his bottle
            helps herself to the tobacco from his pouch

Pavlos
      with a brick in his gut
      turns to sit on a stone
      facing the horizon

      he pulls a notebook from his jacket pocket
      to pen the pain of broken tongues

He writes:

"I hardly wanna face it
            I've learnt words that are ~~ageless~~ basic
            lost all grammatics
            stumbled over ~~upper~~ lowercases

Tripped into conversations
            with my dislocated limbs
            and my broken phrases

Each one a destination
            if I could just get it fluent
            I would feel like ~~a replacement~~ an oasis

            or a return

            I can taste it

A poet without words—

the great frustration

Still my tongue won't say shit
        I need to talk to my ~~homeless~~ homies
        about our homeostasis

I guess we are mosaics:
        shards of glass
        smashed by the first migrations

I'd kiss her feet
        to show her ~~the hard road~~ how we made it

kiss her eyes
        for the darkness that it came with

kiss her lips
        to show her where my pain lives

Hoping she'd reply:

        'Sweet *Pavlo*
        you could never be ~~replaced~~ erased
        despite the great displacement'

But I'm just another one
        born under a southern sun
        blood from the land of the Spartan drum

Just another one
        talking with a ~~flooded~~ punctured lung
        trying to speak his mother tongue"

Pavlos doesn't realise

this pain is called:

φιλοπατρία[100]

the love of a homeland—

the dirt in his hips

the seeds on his tongue

the hurt on his lips:

the sea in his lungs

Eventually
Sophia returns, smoking her cigarette, puts her arm around
Pavlos and tells him:

"There is one thing I think Socrates got wrong

sweet Pavlos

I don't think the kinds of love
form a *ladder* of love

I don't think we have to experience *Eros*
before we can feel *Filia*
and then see *Filoxenia*
to know *Philautia*"[101]

Pavlos looks like a confused puppy

"I think it is less like a ladder
and more like a wheel

where each kind of love is a spoke
and each can lead us outwards
where we can connect with other kinds of love

or they can lead us inwards
to the centre

to the ultimate love…

agapi"

At that moment
    Pavlos and Sophia realise
    that from the very start
    the earth beneath them has been gently beating like a drum

        throbbing like the atrium of a heart

And it's not the screams of protestors
    tear gas canisters
    or the sirens of cop cars

    but something deeper in the dirt:

            the pulse of a dormant star

            Droum droum

                drrouum droum

    It gets louder

            and a mist of silence

                descends over the riot

                Drrouuum

                    Drrroouumm

Police drop their shields

        the people stop their fighting

Droum droum!

drrouum droooouum![102]

though the fires stay ignited
        the city falls quiet…

Back in ancient Athens
   Agathon becomes anxious
   Plato chokes on the seed of a pomegranate
   silence falls over the banquet

Diotima stops kissing Socrates
   in the distance
   she can see the Acropolis is lathered
   with a dim-lit viscous
   and particulates of matter

In an instant she convinces whoever listens
   to stumble up there to find out
   what, in the name of Zeus, is happening[103]

For the first time that night
   the guests of the Symposium
       stand up
       and step out of Agathon's house

and their city of Ancient Athens…

is covered in neon haze and smoke.

The Ancient Greeks see
    staring back at them from the street
    protesters and police
    modern citizens
    bullet proof vests
    boots on their feet

The Modern Greeks see
    figures adorned with robes
    men in leather sandals
    Diotima draped in linen sheets

And for each modern woman
    an ancient twin sister appears right in front

    Two fathers
    of the two eras
    with their two little sons
    start to cuss

The modern man says:

        "what the ffff…."

Both the boys interrupt:

        "Baba! Baba! Μοιάζουν με μάς!
        They look just like us!"

The Moderns see:
    columns, cobblestones, and urns
    statues and marbles iridescently returned
    Socrates, Plato & Aristophanes
    and a hundred more living artefacts and anomalies

The Ancients see:
    men with batons and fatigues
    kids in black hoodies and jeans
    and a thousand more impossibly futuristic entities

Stavros
    breathes again
    and takes of the mask
    Giorgos helps him
    to stand back up
    the blood on their hands, glowing in the dark[104]

    the lines on their palms / *reconfiguring*

Socrates and Diotima
        notice
        the bodies
        of both epochs
        pulsating
        with
        lustre

        They take each other's hands
        and lead the Athenians
        ancient and modern
        up the slopes
        towards
        the
        Acropolis

Back on the Areopagus
        the elders council of 416BC
        covered in dust
        clad in beige robes and wrinkled skins
        are breathing down the necks
        of the people
            who had gathered
                on the sacred granite

Sophia whispers:

        "Something has shifted"

Pavlos whispers:

        "Holy Sh..."

Pavlos and Sophia
        look out across the horizon
        and rise to join the glimmering citizens
        flowing towards them from all over the city
        like a swarm of fireflies

On the Acropolis behind them
        there is a light
        at the top of her stairs
        beckoning the whole city,
        onto her shoulders

            like a call to prayer

Chaos and Cosmos watch on

as the phosphorescent souls

march towards the light

from above

Athens

looks like a wheel

with all of her spokes

finally

leading

inwards[105]

Chapter Eighteen
Ακρόπολις | Acropolis

At the summit

    Pavlos and Sophia

    Socrates and Diotima

    and all the beaming beings

    see:

King Ptolomy
    telling a joke to Hippocrates
    Pythagoras sitting in the dirt
    drawing two perfect isosceles

Aristotle
    leaning on a stone writing quotes
    Pericles taking notes
    on the first democratic vote

Saint Paul and the Ephesians
    meeting with Spartans
    and Mycenaeans
    while walking alongside
    Ottoman soldiers and Venetians

Odysseus
    is trying to chat up two young Parisians
    while Prometheus
    is playing with a flare
    he was just given by some dissidents

▣▣▣▣▣▣▣

The great light

        that they've all come to see

                        hangs above them

    It is a cloud of luminous dust

        and grit

    that circulates and shifts

                that   s h i m m e r s

                    and vibrates

        that churns

                        and   spins

Made up

    of ripped plastic bags

            and used syringes

      chewed up old mixtapes,

         empty tear gas canisters and squashed lids

Remixed

    with all the forgotten flakes

     of bone and skin:

       of Athena's eyelashes

     the dandruff of the masses

     a molecular molasses

       ashes from the mausoleums

It dances and thrusts

like
a
flock   of   starlings

                        rising
                        and
                     falling

at the dimmet of dusk

                     / a murmuration of pure love

As they look above their heads

the people's own bodies

grow brighter

And the cloud

slowly

starts to revolve in a circle:

a gigantic halo

the size of the Parthenon

orbiting around the head of the city

It shines

        brighter and brighter

And the people radiate

        faster and higher

Until the light of the people

and the light of the cloud above them…

touch.

Peasants and adolescents
    become one
    with pigments of graffiti

Every breath
    becomes luminescent
    every piece of rubble
    glows incandescent
    every column starts beaming

Sophia and Diotima's faces
    are painted in a million ways:
    Aspasia
    Hypatia
    Hipparchia
    a slave of Alexander the Great

Sappho and her craft
    Artemis with a bow in her arms
    a bone and all of its parts
    dissolves into the moans of a star

They become miniature
    chiseled and carved
    into the marble of a temple's facade

Every woman is a speck of dust flailing
    and a goddess in the making

Past becomes present
    eons become fractions

The city of Athens
    hurtles through space on an axis
    like a Molotov cocktail hitting a cop on his back

Parthenon scaffolding melts into molten steel
    olive trees turn back into chlorophyll

Police guns and bullets
    fuse together and seal
    the barrels and the triggers
    liquify and congeal

They
    spill out of their holsters

dripping upwards

    dissolving

    into the great

        halo

        of light...

Chaos and Cosmos

lean in to one another

and bear witness

as the people

of all times and places

take the same deep breath

and open

one

unified

mouth.

Chapter Nineteen
Αγάπη | Agapi

Rapping[106]:

"*Agapi* lives
in every piece of dirt on the earth

The cells of our universe
    our lashes
    and our lips
    our skins
    and the moment of our birth

Αγάπη is the sea
    the whales
    the pearls
    the waves as they curl
    the winds as they whirl

As butterflies emerge
    the ferns they unfurl
    the colour on the birds
    the rivers as they merge

The singing of a dirge
    Athena's Owl sitting on her perch

        a lost child returns: Αγάπη is the word

Have you heard?
    Agapi is the surge in the isthmus
    our chance at existence
    our chants of resistance

The stitches
    of the blankets
    that warm us in the winters
    everything we are in an instant

It's in all that is
    and everything that isn't
    the journey through our hearts
    on a search for forgiveness

The black sheep and the herd
    frankincense and myrrh
    the blessings within the curses
    –the lessons we're yet to learn

Αγάπη is the star
    that directs every sailor
    towards their true north
    on a search and a prayer

It is in the night sky
    the bright constellations
    those spirals we find
    in our quiet conversations

The building blocks of us
    the stuff that makes us up
    the cells in our blood
    the love that makes us love

Everything below and above
   Everything below and above

         made of love

"*Agapi* is in the mending
   of a bone that's been broken
   the instinct to heal
   exists in all our open wounds
   that we suffered
      now we hardly remember:

Αγάπη is the bridge
   between our pains
   and our pleasures

A seed in the desert
   waiting on a change in the weather

The love between
   book and professor
   loose change and beggar
   survival and surrender

The splendour
   of a sun set
   on the last day
   of December

All we cannot see
   we begrudge
   all that's dying in the dust
   everything we tried to trust

Everyone they say to hate:
    still made of this kind of love

all that's real or fake:

        the pigeon

            the dove

New shoots gonna grow when you cut that tree

        enemies become friends

        when they find a bigger enemy

        the universe twists and bends

        according to destiny

        fueled by an energy

            that goes beyond you and me[107]

We hang in the balance of gravity

        we gravitate to each other

        based on luminosity

we orbit around the sun

'cause she's the one shining

when we shine

Αγάπη

l o v e

b e c o m e s

r e a l i t y"[108]

ΤΕΛΟΣ

-

THE END

Σημειώσεις του Χάους | Chaos' Notes

[1] I am the black hole, the hollow of the vase, the space within the frame of every window. I know your spaces, too.

[2] God of the tangible, the filling of space, the bridge between the unseen and the seen, the creator of things. My love.

[3] *Oo-ra-nos,* the god of earth's blue ceiling - he knows my eternal name.

[4] It was a smart terracotta pot that figured that one out.

[5] O Agora; altar of human gossip, jewellery stall flirtations and kisses behind council chambers.

[6] Such a fertile smile for marbled Athens to erupt from!

[7] Dionysus could turn a philosophical dinner into a raucous orgy with the tip of a wine-heavy kylix.

[8] The nectar discovered at my nephew Zeus' wedding, a sticky kind of gourmet, now spewed from the mouth of a few billion descendants of the very first bee. Μέλισσες we call them.

[9] Tonight being *The Symposium,* as remembered by Πλάτων in 375BC - by the human numbers. Yesterday, we say.

[10] And I am shrouded in all of them. Soaked in all of them. Doused in all of them. Seeped in all of them. Drowning all things, in everything they are.

[11] Έρως, (*eh-ros*) the romantic type love. A simple kiss is made of *eros,* though some kisses can feel like rotting dead fish-lust, and are not so much *eros* as they are succubus. From the right set of lips, though, a kiss on the cheek can make your fragile vessel implode.

[12] Στοργή, (*stor-yee*). The love of mother and baby, or child and elder. A love that grows between the ill and their carers, with the passing of older

generations or the welcoming of the next.

[13] Φιλοξενία (let it pass your lips like: *feelo-kse-neeya*). The love of the other. We bore its roots in *The Odyssey* - the Cyclops doesn't show *Filoxenia* to Odysseus' men. Instead of feeding them, he feeds on them. This is the true mark of the monster.

[14] Φιλαυτία (*Fil-af-teeya*), 'self-love'. A bubble bath, a nourishing meal for one, a year without seeing another human.

[15] Φιλία - you should say it like *Fil-ee-ya*: Friendship. You know that love that lasts longer than all of your lovers? The one who was there for the first date, the wedding, two births, the divorce and the depression, feeding you whiskey the whole time, showing you Φιλία.

[16] Πράγμα (*Prag-ma*). The love of those lovers who've been together so long that their minds, spirits and histories have fused, become tangible, pragmatic, of the earth.

[17] Αγάπη - pronounced with a soft 'g' and a sharp 'ee': *A-gup-ee*, and never as 'A-gup-paay', don't mess it up, you little fudge figurine. I love you.

[18] This is the real ladder. Plato was mistaken, overshadowed by Diotima's greatness, he reduced her ladder to a few steps and fell off it himself in the process. Agapi is imminent and omnipotent.

[19] This city is demolished and rebuilt, the small-time gods killed and resurrected, pride blooming and flailing, at every second and on the same block.

[20] Ah Agathon, my favourite host, and not a bad poet. Better than Plato, who discarded more detail than he kept. Never let a scientist try to define a soul.

[21] Exarchion Square is actually triangular. And these bitumen beings think they invented geometry.

[22] In *Exarcheia*, squats, anarchist hideouts and radical ideas live between felafel spots, soup kitchens and backgammon championships. My type of place, Cosmos did well.

²³ Golden Dawn, Χρυσή Αυγή, have done something vapidly human - turned fear into power, again. Typical of walking swamps.

²⁴ You are resting well, little Alexandros - your *Kleos* is strong, they still speak your name. Still throw rocks in your honour.

²⁵ I yearn for this feeling again. I might leave Cosmos to do his work and find myself a forest nymph.

²⁶ That's us. Lucky girl.

²⁷ My followers find me on their doomful days. They are the golden few. Humans with godly tastes. Gums full of reverence. Tongues of purple amethyst.

²⁸ Oh to carve a silhouette into the spirited sky!

²⁹ Hail the mysterious one! Praise the name! It means 'She who is honoured by (my nephew and original lady-killer) Zeus'.

³⁰ One of his names is 'Dios', how do you think 'Diotima' came to be?

³¹ *Philo* = 'lover' and *sophia* = 'wisdom'. So *philosopher* = lover of wisdom. In this way there are infinite types of love, if you can do the math my little peloponnesian peninsula - Can you read patterns? The Greeks settled on seven and thought it was enough - some of you depraved little clay sculptures only have one! Ha! Imagine, only having one word for Love! A catastrophe.

³² Χαχαχα. If I was jealous I would have struck lightning on his back in the middle of the act. Socrates, you clump of talking mud, you're lucky that she chose you!

³³ A chant heard from the mouths of angst-ridden emo-apocalyptic teenagers in underground radio shows and clandestine youtube channels across the city, it bounces off the gutters and lands on the laps of a Prime Ministers luncheon, where it is flicked onto the floor like a dead fly.

Sometimes, it ricochets across the apartment buildings and rings in the ears of the youth, giving them hope that their voices matter. It is both insignificant and irreplaceable.

³⁴ Shards of Corinthian columns used to bless the marriage of cop to concrete, of poor Athenian to his historical rage.

³⁵ ἔχουμε πόλεμο ρε γαμώτη! Some of these 'civilised' humanoids really are barbaric! I adore it when they make a nice little war cry against themselves. It's just so cute. The mudbrick mortals look so similar from a distance, to us gods they're only ever just screaming in the mirror.

³⁶ Carved from marble it has him holding a scroll and wearing a helmet - neither of which helped him during the Plague of Athens, Rest In Pandemic.

³⁷ Τζαμί Τζιστωράκη, the Ottoman Mosque sits at the edge of Monastiraki. These two human histories cannot be extracted from each other, though they try. "Greece was Turkey", "Turkey was Greece…", blah blah blah. Just call it Gurkey and be done with it. Names don't exist, only beginnings and ends and these boxes used to prop up the illusion of separation won't last long enough to bother fighting over them. But you can't see that while you're breathing dirt, can you?

³⁸ These little peat puppets of Prometheus do make for interesting inventors. They built a tower and using the water falling off the cliffs of the Acropolis, it attempts to count the uncountable - my very patient primordial acquaintance: *Chronos*.

³⁹ It's also where the Apostle Paul preached about Jesus and monotheism, spreading 'unity' and 'harmony' and all the other precursors to christian dogma. *Death to the non-believers!*

⁴⁰ Told you.

⁴¹ I still find it strange how our little adobe action figures celebrate birth so enthusiastically, but don't enjoy death! A beautiful death is the greatest of honours! Just ask Achilles and his heel.

⁴² I mean, it *was* Aphrodite's birthday party, half the party got pregnant that night.

⁴³ Penìa and Pònos, two godly lovers who are the very definition of opposites attract.

44 Tell me about it, I've had lovers; demigod and mortal, and I still can't keep my thunderous undulations to my partner's constellation.

45 These *Rembetes* used to sing "My lover's eyes shine like the flowers in her garden" in voices that sounded like gravel mixed with granite. Sophia's version is much more soothing.

46 Θεά, Goddess, the female of the godly species. I feel sorry for those allocated only one gender from Cosmos. What a limited existence.

47 The Arab vessels made this word first; it means *'peacefulness'*. For the Greeks it means 'Holy Shit!'. Same, same.

48 The village of Diakofto, that is. He was building the Diakofto to Kalavryta Mountain Railway, known as οδοντωτός - 'the toothed one'.

49 Ahh, Αφροδίτη, how we love you.

50 Whether you pray to Christ, Copulation or Coca-cola - you've only ever prayed to me.

51 Στοργή – the kind of love that chews food for the sick and feeds it to them like birds in spring.

52 This is how a pile of sand with a heart becomes immortal!

53 Διοτίμα was a prophetess. A seer. We left little of her for you to steal. Kept her mystery. Her emptiness. A hole in her form. Be drawn towards her unknown. This is how her legacy is remembered. With great gaping potential. Only a poet can fill the gaps.

54 Her home was all dirt floor and timber, outdoor oven fire pit and murmuring coals, a stone altar with burning Sulphur, wasps hovering about the hanging meat and pine needles tiling her garden.

55 I don't know which igneous rock discovered that squeezing a Phoenician sea-cucumber to death would create a purple dye called Tyrian Purple, that royalty would pay a fortune to wear. Great job, lunatic fisherman with the heavy hands.

⁵⁶ The Beautiful Black Abyss that I am, is the same one her son was born from.

⁵⁷ Past tense. War is a wondrous phenomenon. The humans think they need it to cleanse the bloodlines. To sharpen the focus. To practice gratitude for the days of silence. He passed, tense, on the battlefields - they sing him the hymns of conquest.

⁵⁸ When the guts of the deceased are stretched between two points the humming of planets can be heard in the vibration of their dead spirit.

⁵⁹ A word us gods created to confuse the non-Hellenic speaking jugs. It cannot be translated, but when you feel it, you'll know. And then you won't be able to tell anyone what you felt, without using the same word: *Filotimo.*

⁶⁰ The stones dance this dance of loss and love. Both lament and intense celebration. Originally a bladed duel to the death between the revolutionary militia: the *Zeybeks*. Women have since taken it as their silent, sensual, rebellion.

⁶¹ 'Plato', as you humans know him, was born 'Aristocles' in the same year Pericles died: Rest In Parthenon. Πλατών, *Plato* was just a nickname, it meant 'broad shouldered' - which he apparently had. This Aristocles is our new and improved version, we keep updating the people, same shells, but cleaner souls.

⁶² I love when our little moody marbles make new things. Half *Lo-fi*, half *Boom Bap*, Low Bap is as emo as hip-hop gets, a bit like Tupac's last night in Las Vegas.

⁶³ You know the ones, the students who were sitting on the gates of the university when the military sent a tank straight through their burgeoning youth.

⁶⁴ When a youth's παρέα is made up of lost souls. They must carve his own path towards something greater, even find a whole new family. Like Zeus did to the Titans. We planned it that way. Without the lost souls there cannot be the found, or the finding.

⁶⁵ My favourite place to listen to the amphoras sing my hymns. An open-air Amphitheatre latched onto the side of the Acropolis precipice.

[66] Ἅγιος Παῦλος - Saint Paul lives again! (and again).

[67] You do know Poseidon is my nephew? It can be arranged.

[68] The dirt will take care of your bones, but have some gold ready so we can take care of your soul. Some of you can't even fork out a single coin to cross a river. Heed my words, never be a tightarse in death.

[69] Under their armour they're covered in *gloios*: sweat, battleground dust and the olive oil they've rubbed on their skins before battle. A sacred kind of stink, licked off their pecs by their lovers upon return.

[70] Where the Hellenic heroes and well-favoured mortals live out an immortal afterlife. At least that was before the Christians stole the idea, decided they couldn't afford the spiritual real estate and sold you the lie of some imaginary gated community up in the clouds. And you bought it. Even in death they keep building fences. Relentlessly alone.

[71] Each generation must kill or be killed by the previous, it is an act of honour: the skills taught coming back to teach. The mentor must take pleasure in knowing he will one day be defeated by the student!

[72] Praise be to the sparkling blue of the Aegean. The oily hue in the slick black hair of Hector. The mosaics of Alkínoös' palace. Crushed Lapis Lazuli: eyeshadow of Cleopatra.

[73] Surely they've crossed into the next level, these young lovers, when a neck gets kissed in the middle of a casual hug, *Aman*.

[74] Get a cave already.

[75] We didn't 'dive into his cerebral cortex', we are his cerebral cortex. Our love-juice made him.

[76] How she is still a virgin, I'll never know. Only Cosmos can tell us. Even Zeus couldn't plant his flag.

[77] If he's old enough to come, he's old enough to fight!

[78] Aww sweetheart, maybe no fighties today okay. Just have a wittle rest.

[79] This dog is a warrior on the front line at every protest. True story, google it. Question: Does the man still own the dog if the dog is braver than the man?

[80] She also learned that Ares kisses better than her hunchback husband, but that's a story for another time.

[81] Mastication (as opposed to what you thought I said) began when a fine china teapot with arms from the island of Chios was so hungry he stabbed a pine tree with his spear and chewed on the tasty resin, the nymphs of the forest kept him chewing for an eternity as punishment for hurting their kin. That resin is called μαστίχα: *masticha*.

[82] When old men can no longer climb mountains, pick fruit or till soil. When their knees start to buckle and laughter becomes a wheeze - they come here. Everyday. They see each other's cardigans disintegrate into burial shrouds. If shit-talking was a degree, the Kafeneio would be the university. Some say that it's unfair that the men get to hang out all day while the women stay home. But it is the women that send them there, day after day - to get them out of their way.

[83] ϱε γαμώτο: *you fuck* (unofficial translation).

[84] Because they only lift a finger to point it towards their own navels.

[85] *Kottabos*: A ridiculous drinking game invented by the earthenware dining sets where they'd throw their dregs of wine at a target in the centre of the room and drink only if they missed. Which was most of the time. Presumably the task got harder as the night got older. Hilarious.

[86] A prostitute, just call her a prostitute, it's nothing to be ashamed of you highly articulate emotional infant. Sometimes I really can't believe Cosmos made you from my sacred spew.

[87] Temple of the softest skins! Hallowed halls of sweat and sweet lips! The columns were carved from the breasts of Aphrodite Areia herself!

[88] There is no shame in spiralling closer to your disintegration. Every roof tile one day melts back into the mud. Every one of you monoliths will give your masonry dust back to me for recycling.

[89] Oh Λυκαβηττός! The highest point in Athens, placed by the hands of my great niece, Athena and named 'the one that is walked by wolves'.

[90] The Agora has been rebuilt to perfect scale, but the marble reeks with the blood of the people. The screams of the populace seep from the pores of the rock. These fragile democracies the humans have built are in peril. I much prefer a good old polyamorous dictatorship.

[91] I once shape-shifted into a waitress in *Thisseio* and cornered one of her regulars in the alleyway behind the shop. He was thankful for my visit, obviously. You're welcome, Mr double strength frappè no milk.

[92] Φιλία - affection between friends. Sometimes it leans towards Eros but neither one wants to admit it, until they're naked.

[93] Φίλε - A word that speaks like *friend* but sounds like *brother*. That calls out across the din of night. That links the two in an orbit of gravity. That pulls them close enough to ride together, to crash together, and to keep riding. To mimic molecular momentum.

[94] The tobacco pipes of the Mediterranean. Some call it *Shisha*, some call it ναργιλέ, some call it donating a lung. I saw them, Giorgos and Stavros, lamenting lost loves, calling every frenemy a *malaka*, sharing that copper pipe together. I can tell you now, they never wiped that mouthpiece.

[95] They rode out on that μηχανάκι for a decade. Stavros always hanging off the back. Giorgos always driving in zig-zags and silver muffler snakes. Doing a sign of the cross with one hand when an ambulance passed, steering with a cigarette in the other. Stavros would tell him, *we'll be next if you don't stop being so damn Christian.* They rode it up to the monasteries and smoked joints with the monks. They rode it to the edge of oblivion and peeked over the cliff. They came off a few times, came close to coming back to me. But we let them stay. Let them lean into each new turn.

[96] Imagine. Cosmos placed the earth-juice in the underworld to feed the machinations of Hades. Now the sludge monkeys wage wars over πετρέλαιο, using more of it than they'll gain from winning. Petrol is not cheap anymore. And debt hasn't been forgiven here since the days of Solon.

[97] Patroclus took the hero's armour. He ran towards death to prove himself worthy of love. But a shield cut from a sail will make sure both sink. He

was mistaken for his lover. A tongue forged in bronze is never broken. What can a sand dune do? He must take back the beauty that was stolen.

98 When a lover dies, they are always wearing the scent of those they loved. The mask of the ghost they both became. They take with them a layer of their lover's skin.

99 We were busy birthing a galaxy. Your archaeologists only found half of Diotima's song. Without us, your history, your narratives, your entire existence is an approximation.

100 *Filopatria:* the love of the land - so often grotesquely turned into the love of the flag.

101 She's getting to the good bit now, this Diotima reincarnate. The priestess has returned!

102 The air is gently buzzing like the wings of a hummingbird, the intergalactic conduit has been plugged in, switched on. You're welcome.

103 I could tell you, but I'd have to pulverise you with a whisper. Don't fret, it happens to every cloud of walking dust eventually.

104 When you find *Ichor* running in your veins, enlightenment stuck to your palette. Ready yourself, mud biscuit, to speak.

105 Inwards. Why are you all so scared of your own sacred hollows?

106 Those eloquent antiques. Those fire-breathing libraries. Ready to burn like the books of Alexandria. Hands stitching worlds together. Each gesture a storm. Mouths as open as sky, tongues straight as temple steps. Those Rhapsodes of eternity. Keep weaving your yarns. Keep threading us into your tapestry.

107 The journey from earth to sun is 108 times the sun. The journey from earth to moon is 108 times the moon. Walk into the light. Become the eclipse. Annihilate yourselves in the dawn.

108 Now you're getting somewhere, my slivers of ceramic sentience, now you're getting somewhere.

ABOUT THE AUTHOR

Luka Lesson is a poet, rapper and educator of Greek heritage born in Australia. A former Australian Poetry Slam Champion, Luka has featured at the mecca for slam poetry: the Nuyorican Poet's Cafe (NYC), performed with the Queensland Symphony Orchestra and toured with respected UK rappers Akala and Lowkey.

Luka has released three collections of poetry independently: *The Future Ancients* (2013), *Antidote* (2015) and *Agapi & Other Kinds of Love* (2022) as well as two poetic rap albums: *Please Resist Me* (2012) and *EXIT* (2014).

Luka has facilitated writing workshops in education centres globally, amplifying countless marginalised voices in the process. Luka's poems and rap verses are being studied on official school curriculums throughout Australia, and unofficially by rebellious educators worldwide.

In 2018, Luka established the production company *The Future Ancients*, which produces creative works with a focus on reinvigorating ancient texts in modern ways.

Academically, Luka holds a Bachelor of Arts in Anthropology (UQ), a First-Class Honours in Indigenous Studies (Monash University), and a Masters in Sound Design (Performance Poetry, VCA).

www.lukalesson.com | www.thefutureancients.com